Lizzie McGuire

New Kid in School

Adapted by Jasmine Jones
Based on the series created by Terri Minsky
Part One is based on a teleplay
written by Melissa Gould.
Part Two is based on a teleplay written
by Nina G. Bargiel & Jeremy J. Bargiel.

EGMONT

First published in the USA 2003
by Disney Press
First published in Great Britain 2003
by Egmont Books Limited,
239 Kensington High Street, London W8 6SA

Published by arrangement with Disney Press,
114 Fifth Avenue, New York, New York 10011-5690

Copyright © 2003 Disney Enterprises, Inc.

ISBN 1 4052 0512 1

3 5 7 9 10 8 6 4 2

A CIP catalogue record for this title is available from the British Library

Printed and bound in the UK

Lizzie McGuire

PART ONE

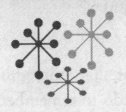

CHAPTER ONE

"Lizzie, there's something I was supposed to tell you," David "Gordo" Gordon said into the phone. "I just can't remember what."

Lizzie McGuire frowned as she played with the leopard-print pillow on her lap. She and her two best friends, Gordo and Miranda Sanchez, were having their usual three-way, before-school gabfest. Lizzie wished Gordo hadn't told her that he'd forgotten to tell her something. Now she'd spend the whole day wondering what that "something" was! And waiting for Gordo to remember things could take a long time.

"Oh, I know!" Miranda chimed in. "Was it about Lizzie's outfit? 'Cause it's, you know, not her fault red's not her color."

"Maybe because it clashed with the green spinach that was in my teeth all afternoon!" Lizzie cried, shuddering. Ugh, she thought, why did I ever think that I could have a spinach salad for lunch yesterday and get away with it?

"Is that what that was?" Gordo asked.

"I thought it was licorice," Miranda said.

Lizzie gaped at the receiver. Were her friends serious? Didn't they know that it was their duty to keep her from looking like a dweebaholic? "That doesn't matter!" Lizzie shouted. "The point is, you're my best friends. You should have told me."

Just then, the door to Lizzie's room swung open. Lizzie sat up straight on her bed, hugging the leopard-print pillow. Her annoying little brother, Matt, was standing in the doorway, cracking up. Lizzie's radar went off. Anything Matt found funny was, by definition, bad news.

"What, dog breath?" Lizzie said.

Matt just cracked up more. "Nothing."

Lizzie wanted to wipe the stupid grin off his face. She grabbed the pillow and tossed it at his head. Matt gasped and pulled the door closed just in time to avoid the assault.

"Freak!" Lizzie called after him.

"That's it!" Gordo said suddenly. "I just remembered what I'm supposed to tell you. Ethan said that if you wanted to sit with him at lunch today, he'd be cool with it."

"Ethan?" Lizzie asked, practically squealing. "Ethan Craft?" Ethan Craft was the most popular guy at Hillridge Junior High School, not to mention the absolute hottest. "He said I can eat lunch with him today? And you're telling me this *now*? *Way* into the conversation? With no time to prepare?" Lizzie looked down at her outfit—her favorite multicolored sweater and orange patterned pants. Not *too* bad. Maybe it wouldn't be her first choice as something to wear to have lunch with Ethan, but it would have to do. Thanks to Gordo's slow memory circuits, she didn't have time to pull together a totally new outfit.

"I couldn't remember," Gordo said defensively. "You want to know why? Because it's not that important!"

Lizzie snorted. "Not important?" she said.

"Gordo," Miranda said, "if Lizzie has lunch with Ethan, the whole school will notice."

"No, they won't," Gordo said.

Lizzie's mouth widened in shock. Not

because Gordo wasn't getting the magnitude of this whole Ethan Craft lunch thing—he never understood stuff like that—but because she had just realized that she had a problem on her hands—the phone was stuck to her ear. Only one person could be responsible for this: her weaselly brother, Matt. He had smeared honey all over the cordless phone, and now it was fastened to her head in a gooey mess.

"Yes, they will," Miranda went on, oblivious to Lizzie's struggle with the phone. "Which translates into being popular. Lizzie will be popular! Which means, *we* will be popular!"

"Whatever," Gordo said with a sigh.

Lizzie struggled to pull the phone away from her head. No luck. She decided to give it a good yank. Unfortunately, she pulled a little too hard, and wound up falling off the bed. *Thunk!*

"Lizzie?" Miranda said into the phone.

"What happened?" Gordo wanted to know.

Lizzie struggled to her knees. "Let's just say I have a problem. It's about four feet tall, it has brown hair, and it's far worse than your not telling me I had spinach stuck in my teeth all afternoon." She struggled with the phone a little more, but it remained fastened to her hair. "I'd hang up," she said, "but I can't."

Matt must have been switched at birth. My real brother couldn't be some prank-pulling, lizard-killing, make-believe-friend-having weirdo. I want a blood test!

Lizzie finally managed to pry the phone from the side of her head and click off. But her ear was still totally sticky. Gross! Now she was going to have to get this goo out of her hair—she didn't have time for a whole new shower—and she'd probably be late for school. Lizzie just hoped that the honey would come out. She couldn't possibly have lunch with Ethan looking like she'd walked face first into a beehive.

Grrr.

How did her little brother manage to be so incredibly annoying? It wasn't possible that they had the same genes.

Lizzie found her mom in the kitchen.

"Mom!" Lizzie yelled. "Look at what Matt did to my hair!" She pointed to the gooey side of her head.

"Oh, dear," Mrs. McGuire said. She motioned to a stool and had Lizzie sit down; then she hesitantly began to inspect the damage. "I don't think it's *too* bad," Lizzie's mom said. "Here, lean back."

She had Lizzie lean backward over the kitchen sink and used the sprayer to wash out the mess. Then she ran upstairs for a small towel and a mirror. "See?" Lizzie's mom said as she rubbed the wet patch of Lizzie's hair dry. She showed Lizzie her reflection in the mirror. "You're as good as new. No big deal."

"No big deal?" Lizzie demanded. "No big deal? But I'm supposed to have lunch with—" Lizzie stopped herself. There was only one thing that could possibly make this morning worse, and that was having to deal with her mom getting all misty-eyed over the fact that Lizzie was having lunch with a boy. "I am having a very important lunch today, Mom," Lizzie said, swallowing her impatience, "and now my hair is ruined!"

"Lizzie, I think we got almost all the honey out," Mrs. McGuire said. "I don't think anyone's going to notice."

"Yes they *will*," Lizzie countered, remembering the spinach incident from the day before—"they just won't say anything." Lizzie sighed. Really—couldn't she just have one day, *one day*, in which she went to school and didn't have to suffer utter humiliation?

Just then, Lizzie's dad walked into the kitchen.

"Well, let's ask your father," Mrs. McGuire said brightly. "Sam, look at Lizzie." Mrs. McGuire put her hands on her daughter's shoulders. "Doesn't she look *especially* nice today?" she prompted.

Mr. McGuire poured himself a cup of coffee. "Yeah, she does," he said, not even bothering to look at Lizzie—"especially her earrings." Lizzie's dad was never really awake until he had his first cup of coffee in the morning.

Poor Dad. He tries so hard but, most of the time, he's clueless.

Mrs. McGuire shook her head slightly.

"Uh, I mean, her outfit," Mr. McGuire corrected.

Mrs. McGuire winced and pointed to her daughter's head.

"Of course, your hair," Mr. McGuire said, finally getting it.

Lizzie rolled her eyes. "See?" she said to her mom. Obviously, her dad was totally lying.

"No, it looks nice," Lizzie's dad insisted. "Beautiful, in fact."

"See?" Mrs. McGuire said, as though her husband's opinion was utter proof that

Lizzie's hair was gorgeous. As though she hadn't just forced him into saying so!

Poor Mom. She's got Dad so well trained, she actually believed that.

"I'm telling you, Lanny, the honey thing worked great!" Matt said into the cordless phone as he wandered into the kitchen. "I did exactly what you said, but I used my sister instead of a hamster." He giggled a little, then turned around and gulped hard when he saw his entire family sitting there, staring at him. "Uh, Lanny, I gotta go," he said quickly, clicking off. "Hi!" he said, giving his family an innocent wave.

"If you wanna know what's good for you, you won't talk to me, you won't look at me, and you'll pretend you don't know me," Lizzie snapped at him.

"Forever?" Matt asked. He shrugged. "Works for me."

"Hey, Matt," Mr. McGuire said in a warning tone. "That's your sister. Be nice."

"But she's such an easy target, Dad," Matt said.

"Oh! Let's see if you can say that with your head underneath my foot!" Lizzie screeched, sliding off her stool and stomping toward Matt.

Mrs. McGuire hurried to step between her daughter and Matt. "Okay, that's it," she said, separating them. She pointed her finger at her son. "Matt, you are grounded."

"Yeah," Mr. McGuire agreed. In a low voice, he asked his wife, "What did he do?"

"Her hair," Mrs. McGuire whispered, jerking her head in Lizzie's direction.

"Oh, right." Mr. McGuire nodded.

Lizzie gritted her teeth. She *knew* her father had been lying!

"So what is it this time?" Matt asked in a bored voice. "No TV? No friends over after school?" He thought for a moment, then added hopefully, "No more chicken noodle casserole?"

"I know," Lizzie said suddenly. "Why don't we just send him away," she suggested. "Like, forever."

"That's not a bad idea," her mother agreed.

Lizzie's eyebrows flew up. She hadn't expected her mom to go for her idea so easily. Maybe I should suggest that she give me twenty bucks, Lizzie thought craftily.

"Hey, that's not very nice!" Matt whined.

"Well, you haven't been very nice, either, young man," Mrs. McGuire replied. "Putting honey on your sister's phone." She waved her hands at him, exasperated. "Just go to school. I'll deal with your punishment later."

"Ooh, I'll rush right home," Matt said sarcastically, his eyeballs rolling back into his head.

I wonder if he can see his tiny brain rolling around in there, Lizzie thought.

"Hey, Matt, cool it," Mr. McGuire said sternly. "All right? You better hurry up before you miss your bus."

Matt sighed, and looked at the floor, completely dejected.

He looked so sad that Lizzie actually felt kind of bad for him.

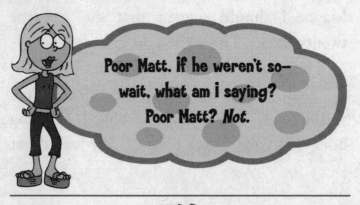

Poor Matt. if he weren't so—
wait, what am i saying?
Poor Matt? *Not.*

"Hey, what about her?" Matt demanded, pointing at Lizzie.

Lizzie planted her hands on her hips. "Mom's taking me to school, brother from another," she said haughtily.

"Ooh, 'Mommy's taking me to school,'" Matt mimicked in an annoying, little-kid voice.

Lizzie narrowed her eyes as Matt left the kitchen. Oh, well. What was the point of getting mad at him now? At least she was going to school, where she would have six whole Matt-free hours . . . not to mention lunch with Ethan!

This day was going to be great. It had "possibility" written all over it.

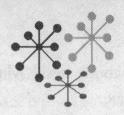

CHAPTER TWO

Matt plodded along toward the bus stop. He was definitely in no hurry to start his day, especially now that he had a punishment waiting for him at the end of it. But as Matt rounded the corner, his eye caught a flash of yellow. The school bus—it was already pulling away from the curb!

"Hey! Hey! Hey, wait for me!" Matt cried, running after the escaping bus. "Don't go!" Matt raced after the bus, his short legs pumping, his heavy backpack bouncing against his shoulder. "Wait!" He chased it for half a block before the driver finally noticed him and slowed down. "Thank you," Matt said as the bus hissed to a stop.

Matt climbed aboard and nodded absently at the bus driver. The bus pulled away as the doors slid shut behind him, and Matt made his way down the aisle, looking for his friends. But he didn't see Lanny or Oscar anywhere. In fact, none of the kids on the bus looked familiar. And most of them looked . . . older.

Suddenly, Matt's eyes grew wide as the truth hit him like a freight train. "Hey," he said out loud, "this isn't my bus!" Matt turned to escape out the front, but it was too late. The bus had already made a few turns. He couldn't possibly get off now. He was on his way to a strange school with a bunch of

eople, and there was nothing he
could do about it!

Just as quickly as he had panicked, Matt
calmed down and realized the situation wasn't
so bad. "Oh, well," he said, sliding into a seat
near the back.

Matt stared out the window, wondering
vaguely where he was headed. The bus jerked
to a stop, and a couple more kids stepped on.

A shadow fell over Matt, and he looked up
into the face of Ethan Craft. Not that Matt
knew who Ethan was. Or that he would have
cared if he had known. But Ethan was pretty
big, compared to Matt, and most other kids
would have been frightened by the look
Ethan was giving Matt at that moment.

"You're in my seat, little man." Ethan
stared down at Matt threateningly. "Move it,"
he commanded.

Matt looked around. There were empty

seats everywhere. "Uh, I don't think so," Matt said.

"You don't think so?" Ethan repeated, glowering at Matt.

"Uh, no," Matt replied. He gave Ethan his most innocent look. "Unless I missed the sign that says RESERVED FOR FRANKENDORK."

Ethan gaped at him. "What?" he demanded.

"Franken. Dork," Matt said slowly, as though he were speaking to an idiot. "Frankendork. I'd show you, but I don't have a mirror."

Ethan glanced over his shoulder as some of the kids behind him started cracking up. "Who are you?" Ethan asked, turning back to Matt.

Matt cocked an eyebrow. "They call me Bond," he said in a cheesy, faux British accent. "Matt Bond."

Ethan frowned. He wasn't used to dealing with extra-small smart alecks on the bus. But he did have a few ideas as to how to handle this one. "All right," he said finally, cracking his knuckles, "you leave me no choice." He pounded his fist into his palm. "How do you want it?" he asked, leaning over Matt menacingly. Most kids shook in their shoes when Ethan threatened to get physical.

But Matt didn't look scared. He just glanced around, then shrugged. "Um, shaken, not stirred?" he suggested, reciting one of his favorite James Bond lines.

That actually cracked Ethan up. "You're funny," he said, laughing and shaking his head.

"So are you," Matt shot back. "But looks aren't everything." He smiled at Ethan.

Ethan grinned. "Slide over, Bond," he said. He wanted to find out what this kid's story was. He was sure that it was going to be pretty interesting.

Lizzie fiddled with her hair as she walked down the hall with Gordo and Miranda later that morning. She still wasn't sure that it looked okay, but she'd managed to do something with it, thanks to a few last minutes with some styling products and a curling iron. She just hoped that it looked good enough for lunchtime with Ethan Craft.

"Your hair looks fine," Gordo assured her for about the fiftieth time. "Really."

"Oh. And for the record, your teeth are clear, too," Miranda chimed in. Her dark hair was looking totally cute in high pigtails fastened with fuzzy pink ponytail holders, and Lizzie tried not to feel jealous that Miranda had a hairstyle that was completely honey-free.

"Thanks, Miranda," Lizzie said, rolling her

eyes. Why couldn't her best friend have given her the tooth update yesterday—when it mattered? Not that Lizzie was going to make a big deal out of it now. She had bigger fish to fry. "Anyway, I've made a decision. I'm not going to let my little brother ruin what is otherwise the greatest day of my entire life."

"What's so great about it?" Gordo asked as he followed Lizzie to her locker.

Lizzie shook her head. Gordo could be so dense sometimes. "Tell him, Miranda," Lizzie said as she yanked open her locker and reached for her English notebook.

"Two words, Gordo," Miranda said.

"If you say 'Ethan Craft,'" Gordo warned, "I swear I'm gonna hurl."

Miranda raised her eyebrows. "Fine," she shot back. "In that case, I'll say one word: lunch."

Gordo made a retching sound and put his

hands to his stomach, like he was going to barf. Lizzie shot him the look of death and slammed her locker shut. Honestly, Gordo could be so immature. But I'm not going to let it bother me, Lizzie told herself. Nothing can ruin this day. Nothing. Not a thing.

As long as my teeth stay clear.

"I hate writing on the chalkboard," Miranda complained to Lizzie as they walked toward their lockers after math class. "It makes my hands all powdery and dry. Like my grandma's face." She looked at Lizzie, who was staring straight ahead, with a dreamy smile on her face. Miranda waved her hand in front of Lizzie's face. "Hello?" Miranda said. "Anybody home?"

"Oh," Lizzie said as she snapped back to reality, "sorry." She gave Miranda an apologetic smile.

"Where is your head today?" Miranda wanted to know.

Lizzie giggled nervously. The truth was, she'd sort of been planning her wedding . . . to Ethan. True, they were only having lunch, but still—weddings take a lot of time to plan. It's best to start early! Not that she wanted to confess that to Miranda. "Oh, nowhere," Lizzie said with a smile.

"Hey, guys," Gordo said as he walked up to them.

"Hey, Gordo," Lizzie said.

"Qué pasa?" Miranda asked.

"Have you guys heard about this new kid?" Gordo asked, frowning.

"You mean the one with the recording contract?" Miranda asked. She looked annoyed. "Yes, I haven't *stopped* hearing about him." She turned to Lizzie and explained. "His parents are spies, he goes to Disney World at least twice a year, and he's already skipped three grades."

"Yeah, well how 'bout the fact that he's already made a movie! A *movie*!" Gordo ranted. "And not just any movie, but a feature film! With Steven Spielberg! And he's younger than I am! He's *younger*"—Gordo pointed to himself—"than me!"

"Whoa, whoa, whoa. Who is this kid, anyway?" Lizzie asked.

"I haven't met him yet," Miranda admitted, "but he's a friend of Ethan Craft's."

"Ethan?" Lizzie asked, giggling slightly. Any friend of Ethan's is . . . well . . . someone I may have to invite to my future wedding! Lizzie thought happily.

"He transferred here from some small, private school on an uncharted island near Fiji," Miranda went on as the three friends headed down the hallway. "His name is, uh, uh,"

Miranda said, scratching her head, thinking hard. "Matt something."

Lizzie froze in her tracks and grabbed Miranda's wrist. "Matt?" she repeated. "Please, don't say that name around me."

"I can't believe it," Gordo went on, clearly not listening to them. "Younger than me and he's already worked with Spielberg."

Just then, a classroom door flew open, whacking Lizzie in the face! Lizzie's papers went flying as she fell flat on her back. A crowd of kids poured out of the room, completely oblivious of Lizzie and her pain.

From her spot on the ground, Lizzie heard a familiar-sounding voice say, "So I said to him, *Harry Potter* should be seen, not just read, and that's why they're making the movie." Lizzie wondered whether the voice belonged to the new kid, as a bunch of other voices chorused their admiration. She was pretty sure that she heard Ethan's voice saying, "Way to go, Bond!"

"Lizzie!" Miranda said, kneeling over her friend.

"Are you okay?" Gordo asked.

Lizzie grabbed her head. "Yeah, I'm fine," she said woozily. "Was that . . ."—Lizzie glanced over her shoulder, but the crowd had already turned the corner—"was that Ethan? Did he say anything about lunch?" she asked hopefully.

Gordo and Miranda just looked at each other.

Okay, Lizzie thought, reading their expressions. I guess you could say that I'm definitely out to lunch!

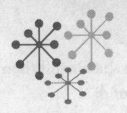

CHAPTER THREE

"Oh, Sam, this is all my fault!" Mrs. McGuire wailed as she hurried into the kitchen, where Mr. McGuire was busy at his computer.

"Hold on a second, honey," Mr. McGuire said. "I'm making a killing on this on-line auction, selling your old Leif Garrett records."

"Sam, I need you to listen to me," Mrs. McGuire said urgently. "It's Matt." Mrs. McGuire's voice was shaking. "He's missing.

His school just called. He never showed up. And the last thing I said to him before he went to school was that I thought that we should send him away forever." Her voice cracked with emotion. "And I think he thinks I hate him, and he ran away from home—I mean, from us, I mean . . ." She swallowed hard, and touched her chest. "From *me*!"

"Now, just slow down, all right, honey?" Mr. McGuire said soothingly. "This has happened before, remember? That time that Matt hid under the bed for an entire day so that he didn't have to do the square dancing during P.E.?"

Mrs. McGuire took a deep breath, remembering. Matt had worn a camouflage hat to blend in with the other junk under his bed.

"No, I checked under the bed!" Mrs. McGuire said. "And the only thing there was a week-old chicken noodle casserole." She bit her lip, holding back tears. "I thought he liked that, too."

"You know, he's gotta be around here somewhere," Mr. McGuire said confidently. "Do you remember the time he sneaked out so he could be the first in line at the toy store to meet Tarzan?"

"Yeah, he didn't sneak out," Mrs. McGuire said sheepishly.

"Huh?" her husband asked.

"I went with him," Mrs. McGuire admitted.

"I knew you liked that guy!" Mr. McGuire cried. "It was the way he was hanging from the rope, right? And the loincloth and all—"

"Okay, okay, okay!" Mrs. McGuire shouted. "This is serious! Matt's missing, and we have to find him!"

"Okay," Mr. McGuire said. "Look, you check the closets. I'll look under the house."

He pushed back his chair and headed out onto the patio.

Mrs. McGuire nodded, then hurried out of the kitchen. She was going to tear apart each and every closet in the house until she found her baby!

"Okay, this is it," Lizzie said excitedly, as she walked into the lunchroom with Miranda—"the moment I've been waiting for, for, like, my entire life. Lunch with Ethan Craft."

Just then, Lizzie spotted Ethan across the cafeteria. He was standing with a group of popular kids. He looked up, and gave Lizzie a nod and a smile.

"I want you to remember every detail," Miranda sputtered eagerly. She was so excited, she was practically sending saliva across the room. "Every expression, every word—"

"No worries, Miranda," Lizzie said, grabbing

Miranda's shoulders. "I'll tell you everything."
She giggled.

"Spank you!" Miranda said, giggling, too.

Just then, Gordo walked up to them, carrying his lunch tray. "Okay, I wasn't going to say anything, but I think you need to hear this," he said to Lizzie. "The fact that you care so much about sitting with Ethan is kind of pathetic." Miranda and Lizzie exchanged glances as Gordo went on with his lecture. "So he's popular," Gordo admitted. "And maybe he's good-looking. So what? Who you are is way more important than who you sit with at lunch."

Lizzie looked him up and down skeptically. "You done?" she asked.

Gordo nodded.

"Good," Lizzie said. "Here I go!" She gave Miranda a hug.

"Good luck!" Miranda chirped.

"Hey, Lizzie, over here!" Ethan called out from his lunchroom table.

Lizzie gulped, picturing herself running toward Ethan on a silver cloud. This was a dream. No, it was better than a dream. It was . . .

The crowd Ethan was standing with let out a cheer. As Lizzie walked up to them, she saw that they were all gathered around an incredibly small kid, who was standing on a table, wiggling his butt. Someone had brought in a boom box, which was blaring dance music. Who is this guy, and what in the world is he doing? Lizzie wondered. Just then, the kid turned around and struck a pose on the table. "And that's how Britney learned to dance!" the kid announced.

Lizzie couldn't believe her eyes. The kid who was wiggling his butt on the table, the kid who was friends with Ethan Craft, was her annoying little brother. *Matt?* she thought. Matt! This was no dream—it was a *nightmare*!

That's when Matt noticed Lizzie. "Ahhh!" he screamed.

"Ahhh!" Lizzie screamed back.

The screaming went on and on.

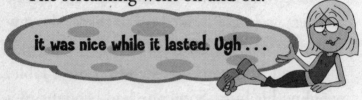

it was nice while it lasted. Ugh . . .

Lizzie grabbed Matt by the front of his shirt and dragged him off the cafeteria table.

"What are you doing?" Matt demanded through clenched teeth as Lizzie led him away from the crowd.

"Getting my life back," Lizzie growled.

"Hey, don't worry," Matt called over his shoulder to the confused crowd of kids that stood watching him get hauled away. "I'll tell you how I was knighted by the queen when I get back." He winked and pointed a finger pistol at the crowd as Lizzie dragged him out the cafeteria door.

"What are you doing here?" Lizzie demanded once they were out in the hall.

Matt thought for a moment. "Well, see, it all started when—"

"Do Mom and Dad know that you're not in school?" Lizzie asked, cutting him off.

Matt gave Lizzie a condescending look. "But I *am* in—"

Suddenly, the truth crashed over Lizzie like a tidal wave, and she gasped. "*You're* the new kid, aren't you?"

Matt shrugged. "Well, it kind of looks that way, but—"

"Does anybody know that you're my brother?" Lizzie asked.

Kate Sanders, the most popular girl in

school, picked that moment to come sauntering by with her posse trailing behind her. Lizzie bit back a groan. Kate had been making Lizzie's life miserable ever since they hit junior high. She and Kate used to be friends, but once Kate became queen bee, she had no more use for unpopular drones like Lizzie.

"Well, at first I thought he did look kind of familiar," Kate said, loud enough for Lizzie to hear as she pranced past, "but then I thought, Lizzie could never be related to anybody that cool and charming." Kate caught sight of Matt and gave him a little wave. "Oh, hi, Matt," she said, batting her eyelashes. Then she turned and strutted into the cafeteria.

Lizzie cringed as her brother gave Kate a casual wave.

"Did Kate just call you 'cool'?" Lizzie asked Matt. Matt cocked an eyebrow and opened his mouth to reply, but Lizzie decided that she didn't want to hear the answer. "Never mind," she said quickly. "Here's the plan, we're gonna call Mom and Dad to pick you up, and by tomorrow, everyone will have forgotten who you are."

"Uh," Matt said slowly, "that's not going to work for me."

"What?" Lizzie gaped at him.

"I like it here," Matt explained. "The playground's bigger, the food's better, and everybody's really nice." Matt waved to some eighth grader who was walking by. "Especially that Ethan guy."

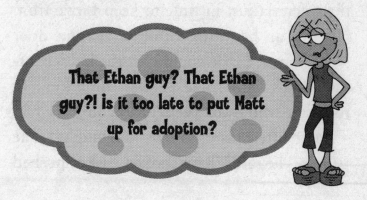

That Ethan guy? That Ethan guy?! is it too late to put Matt up for adoption?

Lizzie glared at Matt, completely speechless. Was he really talking about her lunch date and potential husband that way?

"You know, all I ever hear you say about this place is how horrible it is," Matt went on. "But it's really not. I like it here." He put his hands on his hips. "I'm staying."

"No, you're not!" Lizzie cried, horrified at the very idea.

Matt opened his eyes wide. "Uh, yes, I am," he said in his best *duh* voice.

"No!" Lizzie screeched.

Luckily, Miranda and Gordo walked out of the cafeteria just in time to keep Lizzie from lunging at her little brother. As the door swung open, Lizzie could hear the kids chanting Matt's name, like he was some kind of rock star who owed them an encore.

Matt lifted his eyebrows knowingly. "The people," he said, "have spoken." Matt pushed his way past Miranda and Gordo, and swaggered through the cafeteria doors. A cheer went up as he entered the room.

Gordo stared after him a moment. "At the risk of sounding selfish, I, for one, am glad it's Matt," he said.

Lizzie's jaw dropped open. Had Gordo lost his mind?

"Steven Spielberg," Gordo said, chuckling to himself. "What an imagination."

"So, what are you going to do?" Miranda asked Lizzie.

Lizzie was too stressed to do anything but offer a feeble squeak in reply. But of course—there was only one solution to this problem.

What am i going to do? i'll do what any other red-blooded sibling would do. i'll go to Mom and Dad.

CHAPTER FOUR

Mr. and Mrs. McGuire stood in front of Matt's best friend, Lanny, who was seated on their couch. The McGuires had called the police and half of Matt's friends, but so far, they hadn't heard anything about where their son had gone. A police officer was in the kitchen, trying to get some information from headquarters. Meanwhile, the elementary school had let the McGuires pull Lanny out of class to see if he knew where Matt might be. But so far, the kid was being pretty tight-lipped. Not that that was unusual for Lanny. In fact, neither Mr. nor Mrs. McGuire could ever remember having heard him utter so much as a peep. Then again, Matt spent hours on the phone with Lanny—so they knew he must talk sometimes. Or at least, they *hoped* he talked sometimes.

"So," Mr. McGuire said, "did Matt say anything about not going to school today, Lanny?"

Lanny shook his head.

Mrs. McGuire looked at him accusingly. "You were on the phone with him this morning," she pointed out.

Lanny shrugged.

Mr. and Mrs. McGuire looked at each other, then leaned toward Lanny. "Nothing about square dancing or missing a test?" Mr. McGuire suggested.

Lanny thought for a moment, then nodded.

"Yeah?" Mr. McGuire asked eagerly.

Lanny looked around, reconsidering, then shook his head no.

Mr. and Mrs. McGuire straightened up. "The kid's not talking," Mr. McGuire whispered.

"Does he ever?" Mrs. McGuire demanded through clenched teeth.

"He's one of Matt's best friends," Mr. McGuire said. They both turned to look at Lanny, who had folded his arms across the couch's armrest, and was staring intently at the gnome lamp that stood on the side table.

"That's not saying much," Mrs. McGuire said with a sigh.

Just then, the police officer walked into the living room.

"I just checked with headquarters," he

announced, hooking his thumbs through his belt. "They're gonna circulate some pictures, canvas the area. Don't worry, in cases like this, it's best to just sit tight. We'll know something soon." He glanced over at Lanny, who was still staring at the gnome. Lanny looked up at the officer and cocked an eyebrow. "You're right," the officer said. "Gnomes are weird." Then he shook his head and walked back into the kitchen.

Mr. and Mrs. McGuire stared at each other. Maybe they should have had the police officer question Lanny!

"But they never let us make phone calls from the principal's office," Miranda protested as she walked down the stairs next to Lizzie.

"Are we or are we not allowed to use the school phone in case of emergencies?" Lizzie demanded, not even breaking her stride.

"Allowed," Miranda admitted reluctantly.

"And, being my best friend and knowing how I feel about him, do you or do you not think that Matt's being here is an emergency?" Lizzie asked.

"Well, see," Miranda said uncomfortably, "that's where you and I differ."

Lizzie swung around to look her friend in the eye. "Miranda," she griped, stomping her foot, "it's *Matt*. The best thing about going to school every day is the fact that he's *not* going to be there!"

"But for the first time in our lives, we can use him to our advantage," Miranda insisted.

Lizzie folded her arms across her chest and looked at her friend skeptically. "No, thanks."

"But Matt's a friend of Ethan's," Miranda said, "which makes Matt popular. *We* want to be popular. Matt could help us."

"Help us?" Lizzie couldn't believe her ears.

"He's already ruined my lunch with Ethan Craft. Besides, I don't even care anymore. I just want him gone!"

Miranda nodded, as though she understood, then shook her head. "This all made sense to me before we started talking."

"Well, while you're trying to make sense of it, I'll be in the office, using the school phone," Lizzie snapped. "Later." She turned on her heel and strode away dramatically —colliding face first with an open locker door. She fell to the ground.

"You see?" Matt said as he climbed out of the locker. "As long as you can hold your breath, being stuffed inside a locker isn't really that bad." He turned to two geeks and motioned for one of them to step inside. "Here, you try it." As one geek stepped into the locker, Matt noticed Lizzie glaring up at him from the floor.

"Hel-lo," Matt singsonged cheerfully, giving her a little wave.

Lizzie hauled herself to her feet. Matt didn't hesitate; he turned and ran as Lizzie chased after him. As she ran past the locker, her elbow caught the door, slamming it shut.

Miranda started after Lizzie.

"Um, hello?" said a muffled voice from inside the locker. "Anybody?"

Miranda looked at the locker, then shrugged and kept walking.

Not her brother. Not her locker. Not her problem.

Lizzie walked into the main office and glanced around. Good—the coast was clear. She reached over the front desk and pulled out the phone. She had just picked up the receiver and begun to punch in her home phone number when Principal Tweedy walked out of his private office . . . with Matt. Thinking that her brother had been busted, Lizzie started to smile—then she noticed that there was something definitely wrong with this picture. Principal Tweedy was grinning. And he had his arm around Matt. Not good. Lizzie hid the phone behind her back.

"The way that you've explained it," Principal Tweedy said to Matt, "I see no reason why scooters shouldn't be a part of the P.E. curriculum. I'm gonna bring it up with the board."

Lizzie gulped when Principal Tweedy noticed her. "Now, you know the rules, Ms. McGuire," he said. "No student phone calls."

"But this is an emergency," Lizzie insisted, gesturing toward Matt. "I mean, my little brother's at my school!"

"Yes, he is," Principal Tweedy said as he

patted Matt on the back, "and we're very lucky to have him."

Matt gave Lizzie a triumphant look.

"But he doesn't belong here!" Lizzie cried.

"You're right," Principal Tweedy said. He looked at Matt and smiled. "He belongs in the gifted program."

"You don't understand," Lizzie said, shaking her head.

"Oh, but I do. And just a tip, Lizzie," the principal said, patronizingly—"jealousy isn't pretty on a girl. Let's try and work through it."

Matt started to crack up.

Lizzie decided that it was time to take the direct approach. "Excuse me," she said, holding out the phone to Principal Tweedy. "Can you just call my parents? I'm sure they're really worried about him." Let's see what the principal has to say about my "jealousy" when he gets an earful from Mom, Lizzie thought happily.

"Uh, no," Matt said quickly, patting the principal on the shoulders, "you don't have to do that."

"Actually, I was gonna do that right now," Principal Tweedy said. He held up a Rolodex card and took the phone from Lizzie, who shot Matt a victorious smirk.

"You are so busted," Lizzie whispered as Matt began to bang his head against the desk.

Principal Tweedy finished dialing and waited. "It's the machine," he said after a moment.

Matt lifted his head from the desk. "Yes!" he hissed.

"Hello," the principal said into the phone, "this is Principal Tweedy from Lizzie's school. Just wanted to call and say what a joy it is having Matt here with us today." Matt flashed Lizzie an evil grin.

Somebody, wake me up! Please, anybody, wake me up from this horrible nightmare!

Lizzie gave herself a pinch, but it didn't help. This was really happening. And there was no way out!

Okay, Lizzie thought, the only way to fix this situation is to go to extreme measures. She scanned the hall as she hurried toward social studies class. Bingo. Ethan was just heading into the classroom. And there's still three minutes until the bell, Lizzie thought. Plenty of time to rat Matt out.

"Hi, Ethan," Lizzie said as she slipped into the chair next to his.

"Hey, Lizzie," Ethan said, looking up at her with a smile.

How should I begin? Lizzie wondered, taking a deep breath. She decided to just dive right in. "So, I just thought I should tell you," Lizzie began, jiggling her leg tensely, "Matt's not who you think he is. I just thought you should know that." She let out a nervous giggle, which she hoped didn't sound too dorky.

Ethan's eyebrows drew together. "Weird," he said slowly. "The little guy *said* you'd do something like this."

Lizzie frowned. "He *did*?"

Ethan stared at her.

Please, don't let him be staring at the honey patch on my head, Lizzie begged silently. "Something wrong?" Lizzie asked, giggling nervously again.

"Nah, I was just wondering, does your brain hurt, like, all the time?" Ethan asked.

"My *brain*?" Lizzie asked, rolling her eyes. This conversation was getting majorly weird.

"I never met anybody with permanent brain freeze," Ethan went on. "Mine just lasts, like, a minute."

"What are you talking about?" Lizzie asked. I don't have brain freeze! she thought. Where could Ethan have gotten an idea like . . . ? Wait a minute. "What else did that little Matt say about me?"

"About your eyes," Ethan said, leaning in closer.

Lizzie felt her cheeks get hot. Was it possible that her brother had actually said something nice about her—like, that she had beautiful eyes? Ethan was staring at her so intently, what else could it mean? "What about my eyes?" Lizzie asked hopefully. If Matt said something really nice, Lizzie thought, I might just let him live.

"Does the one really pop all the way out of your head when you get mad?" Ethan asked.

That's it! Matt's going down!

Lizzie was completely speechless. Ethan actually thought that she had brain dysfunction and freakish eyes? Okay, no more Ms. Nice Girl, she decided. It was definitely time to pull out the heavy artillery.

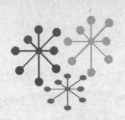

CHAPTER FIVE

Mr. and Mrs. McGuire paced back and forth in the kitchen while the police officer sat at the table, sipping coffee and munching a doughnut. He'd had three already.

"Well, this is ridiculous!" Mrs. McGuire said finally. "I can't stand here, waiting. I'm going nuts!"

"Isn't there something we can do?" Mr. McGuire asked the officer.

"It's best to just stay home and wait for the

phone to ring," the police officer assured him. "Other than that," he added brightly, holding out his mug, "I'd love some more coffee."

"No," Mrs. McGuire shouted. She slapped her hand down on the kitchen table. "No! I'm not making you any more coffee until you can tell me where my baby is!"

All of a sudden, Mr. McGuire remembered what he had done. "Wait a second!" he said. "I turned the phone off when I was on-line and—"

Mrs. McGuire stared at him. "What?" she demanded. "It's been off this whole time?" She ran over to the answering machine.

"Well, I was wheeling and dealing," Mr. McGuire explained defensively, hurrying after her. "You know, 'cause Leif Garrett records are really hot these days." He looked down at the machine, which was blinking. "Oh, look, messages!"

Mrs. McGuire glared at him, then sighed and pressed PLAY. The first message was from Mrs. McGuire's mother. Mrs. McGuire rolled her eyes and fast-forwarded to the next message. "I'll deal with her later," she said.

There was a beep, then Principal Tweedy's voice spilled from the machine. "Hello, this is Principal Tweedy from Lizzie's school—" Mrs. McGuire pressed FAST FORWARD. "Lizzie's school?" she moaned. "I don't have time for you—my baby's missing!" But that was the end of the messages. "That's the last message?" Mrs. McGuire said, sniffling a little. "But I wanted to hear from Matt. I want my Matty!" she wailed, hugging the machine against her chest. "I want my Matty!"

Mr. McGuire wrapped her into a big hug. "Honey, it's going to be okay," he reassured her. "It's gonna be fine."

"Um," the police officer interrupted, pointing toward the kitchen, "that coffee?"

"And voilà," Matt said as he sat on a lab table in Lizzie's science class—"the perfect meal." Matt lifted the lid off a metal crucible and showed off what he had concocted to the small crowd of kids that had gathered around him. They burst into applause. "I'll be sharing more recipes on *Oprah* next month," he told them.

Lizzie sighed and tapped her pen impatiently against her notebook.

"There you are," Miranda said as she and Gordo strode into the room.

"You okay?" Gordo asked, leaning against Lizzie's lab table.

"Never better, actually," Lizzie said with a smile.

"Why the sudden turnaround?" Miranda asked suspiciously.

Gordo leaned against the lab table and frowned. "Yeah, I heard Principal Tweedy busted you."

Lizzie looked at the ceiling and smiled innocently. "It was worth it."

"Say what?" Miranda asked.

"While Principal Tweedy was showing Matt around the school, I sneaked in and used his phone to call—" But Lizzie never finished her sentence, because just then, two uniformed police officers walked into the classroom. She turned around to look at Matt, who was in the middle of yet another one of his stories.

"So I said, 'Tissue? I hardly know you. . . .'" Matt grinned as the crowd of kids cracked up.

The tall police officer looked at Matt dubiously. "Matt McGuire?" he asked.

When Matt saw the policeman, his eyes

went wide. "No," he said quickly in a phony British accent. "No Matt McGuire here."

The officer looked down at the pad of paper in his hand and tried again. "Bond?" he asked. "Matt Bond?"

Matt pressed his lips together. "I guess the jig is up," he said dramatically as he slithered down from the lab table. He placed his hands behind his head. "Go easy on me, would you, fellas?"

Lizzie giggled as the police escorted her brother from the classroom. Talk about getting stone-cold busted!

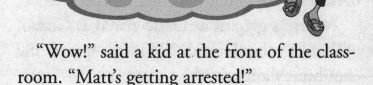

Woo-hoo! Yeah!

"Wow!" said a kid at the front of the classroom. "Matt's getting arrested!"

"How cool!" someone else said. The crowd murmured their admiration as Matt and the police walked out the door.

What? I just can't win today! Now I've made him even *more* popular.

Lizzie groaned and put her head on her lab table.

"Well, you know what they say," Miranda said, her chin in her palm. "Tomorrow is another day."

"That may be true," Gordo piped in, "but Matt's *always* going to be her brother."

Miranda giggled as Lizzie glared at Gordo. "Thanks," Lizzie said. "Way to spread the sunshine, Gordo."

Gordo grinned. Then he shook his head and chuckled. "Spielberg," he said. He slapped the lab table and walked out of the room.

"It's okay," Miranda said, putting a sympathetic arm around her friend. "I feel for you."

Lizzie sighed. Nobody could possibly understand the pain of having Matt for a brother. Nobody. He'd actually managed to destroy a day full of possibilities!

And I thought a little tooth spinach was bad, Lizzie thought. At least she had managed to floss that away. Matt was going to stick around . . . forever!

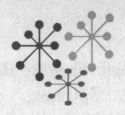

CHAPTER SIX

"**S**o, did Matt get in beaucoup trouble?" Gordo asked later that night when he, Miranda, and Lizzie were on a three-way call.

Lizzie grinned in satisfaction. "Total. Grounded for a month—no TV, no phone, and the best part is, he's got to keep a solid ten feet away from me at all times."

"Yeah, but meanwhile, everyone at school is still talking about him," Miranda said with a sigh.

"Yup, nothing says 'cool' like getting arrested," Gordo chimed in sarcastically. "Especially at school."

Lizzie's phone beeped. "Oh, hold on," she said, "I got another call, guys." She clicked over. "Hello?"

"Lizzie?" someone said. Lizzie's heart started pounding like crazy. She knew that voice!

"Hi, it's Ethan."

"Ethan," Lizzie said, trying to sound as casual as possible. "Hi. Um—can you hold on a second?" She clicked back over to her friends. "Omigosh, you guys," she said breathlessly. "Ethan! It's Ethan Craft. He's on the other line!"

"Ethan?" Miranda squealed.

"Omigosh, I gotta go!" Lizzie said quickly. How many seconds have gone by since I clicked over? Lizzie wondered, hoping desperately that Ethan hadn't hung up.

"Ethan!" Miranda repeated. "Oooh, Lizzie, I so want to be you!"

"Can someone please explain this guy's appeal to me?" Gordo asked, sounding bored.

Lizzie bit back a groan and clicked off. Let Miranda explain it to Gordo. Lizzie had important people to talk to!

"I'm back," Lizzie said to Ethan as soon as she clicked over. Omigosh, she thought giddily. Maybe he wants to ask me to sit next to him at lunch tomorrow, since Matt ruined our plans today! "So, what's up?"

"Hey, listen," Ethan said. "I was wondering. . . . What are you doing for lunch on Saturday?"

Lizzie grinned. Lunch on *Saturday*? Even better. That was practically a *date*! Her heart fluttered. Ethan is asking me out! she thought. "Uh, nothing," she said. "Yet."

"So then you'll have time to . . ."

Lizzie's heart skipped a beat.

". . . pick up a pizza for me and Matt," Ethan finished happily. "I *love* that little guy."

What? Ethan wanted to hang out with . . . Matt? "That'd be, that'd be great," Lizzie snapped, "but I think that's when Matt's nap time is. Later." She clicked off and sighed, throwing her head back. Unfortunately, she threw it a little too far back and fell off the bed. "Ow!" she cried.

Matt ruined the best phone call of my life! it's not over. i'll get him.

"Watch out, little brother," Lizzie said from the floor. "I'll get you . . ." With a sigh she stared up at the ceiling and added—". . . one of these days."

Lizzie McGUIRE

PART
TWO

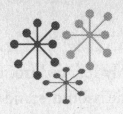

CHAPTER ONE

"**F**ace it, Miranda," Lizzie McGuire said into the phone. It was after dinner and she had been in her room chatting with Miranda and Gordo for the past twenty minutes. "It doesn't matter which X-Man you are. You could be Mystique, that hot blue chick, and Ethan Craft wouldn't give you the time of day. Which is why *I'd* be Rogue. I'd use my mutant power to suck away all of Kate's popularity." Lizzie smiled smugly at the receiver, imagining the scene: her mortal enemy, Kate

Sanders, suddenly reduced from queen bee to wanna-be. Lizzie would stand there triumphantly while Ethan Craft panted at her feet. "Ethan would have no choice but to turn to me."

"Or *moi*," Miranda pointed out.

"Great," Gordo said sarcastically. "Use the untapped powers of the universe to land a guy who's gonna end up working at a gas station. *Part-time*."

Lizzie let out an insulted gasp. Gordo was a good friend, but he was a guy, and he had no appreciation for Ethan's utter hottitude.

Just then, the door swung open behind Lizzie. "Hel-lo? Ever heard of knocking?" Lizzie demanded as her annoying little brother, Matt, strode into her room. He was covered in dirt and carrying a shovel, which was pretty weird—even for him.

"Have you seen the flashlight?" Matt asked

as he yanked open Lizzie's dresser drawers.

"No," Lizzie said, staring at him. She crossed the room and slammed the drawers shut. Lizzie pointed to the phone, which she was still holding to her ear. "On the phone," she singsonged to Matt. "Leave."

Matt pulled open another dresser drawer, and Lizzie finally realized that her X-Man conversation was going to have to wait while she dealt with the dark forces of the universe that had just invaded her bedroom.

"Ugh!" Lizzie groaned into the receiver. "I have to get off the phone and crush my little brother." She clicked off and followed Matt to the other end of her room, where he was investigating the pile of dirty clothes on top of Lizzie's wicker hamper.

He dug through the clothes, tossing them aside recklessly. Lizzie shrieked as a green shirt landed on her shoulder. A moment later, a pair of blue patterned pants flopped onto her head. "You have five seconds till I sit on your head," she told her little brother through gritted teeth. "One . . . two . . ."

Matt continued to dump clothes on the floor, completely ignoring her.

"Three . . ." Lizzie continued.

"Got it!" Matt said cheerfully as he pulled the small black flashlight from the bottom of the hamper, where it had been hidden beneath the pile of laundry. He waved the flashlight in Lizzie's face triumphantly and jogged out the door just as Lizzie's dad wandered in.

"Does anyone knock in this house?" Lizzie demanded as she yanked the pair of pants off her head.

Mr. McGuire flashed his daughter a guilty look, then walked back to the door and rapped on it softly.

"Yes, Dad," Lizzie said with a forced smile as she brushed wisps of hair away from her face. Thanks to the pants that had landed on her head, Lizzie's blond hair now looked like a bird's nest topped with a hot-pink headband. "What do you want?"

"Do you have any idea why your little brother is covered in dirt?" Mr. McGuire asked.

Lizzie folded her arms across her chest. Honestly, why would her dad think that she had any idea why Matt did *anything*? "You caught me," she said sarcastically. "I buried him in the backyard, and he dug his way out."

Mr. McGuire's eyes went wide in shock.

"Joke!" Lizzie cried.

Her dad raised his eyebrows, but Lizzie couldn't tell if he thought the joke wasn't funny, or if he thought she might actually have tried to bury Matt in the backyard.

Come to think of it, Lizzie thought, I wish that I'd had that idea earlier. It has potential.

"I don't know why he's Mud Boy," Lizzie went on, "but I've got a lot to worry about, Dad. I'm getting married in the morning, so would you please excuse me?" Lizzie stormed off as her dad's mouth dropped open.

Mr. McGuire stood in the middle of Lizzie's room, clearly stunned by his daughter's wedding plans. "Honey?" he called weakly to his wife. "I need a little help!"

"The rules for the social-studies marriage project are as follows," Mrs. Stebel said later that morning as she passed out stacks of green handouts to the first person in every row. "I will pair you off into couples, and then everyone will come and select an occupation from this fishbowl." She held up a large round fishbowl that was full of brightly colored slips of paper.

Lizzie and Miranda smiled at each other, then glanced over at Ethan. Lizzie sighed, hoping desperately that Ethan would be her partner for the marriage project. He was just so gorgeous, and he looked even hotter than usual today. His sandy brown hair seemed to glow beneath the fluorescent school lights.

"Each couple must create a fictional lifestyle for themselves," Mrs. Stebel went on as she held up the fishbowl at the front of the room. Lizzie really liked Mrs. Stebel, their social studies teacher. She wore funky clothes and big, dangly earrings, and her hair was styled in supercool shortie dreds. She was always trying to think up creative projects for the class. And, in Lizzie's humble opinion, this project was definitely cool, since it came with the possibility of marrying Ethan! "And the couple with the best marriage *doesn't* have to write a paper," Mrs. Stebel added.

Lizzie lifted her eyebrows and wrote that down in her notebook. She definitely wanted to work hard on her marriage so she wouldn't have to write the paper! On the other hand, writing a paper could, potentially, equal more time with Ethan. . . .

"Each couple must make all decisions together," Mrs. Stebel went on. "The project will last one week and end with a pretend twentieth school-reunion party where you'll give a report about your last twenty years." Mrs. Stebel looked around the room. "Any questions?"

Yeah. Where's my bachelor number one?

The whole class was quiet.

"Okay," Mrs. Stebel said as she settled

behind her desk, "let's begin." She looked down at her notepad. "Kate Sanders."

Ugh, Lizzie thought as she watched Kate sit up eagerly and glance over at Ethan with a confident smile. Kate had gotten dressed up for today's assignment. She was wearing a sparkly white sweater with fluffy feathers at the wrists over a white T-shirt with a silver glitter heart on the front. She even had a sparkly barrette in her hair. Lizzie looked down at her powder blue vinyl jacket. Sure, it was cool, but it didn't really say, "World's Most Perfect Bride," the way Kate's outfit did. Lizzie sighed.

"Kate, you will be married to—" Mrs. Stebel looked down at her notes. Suddenly, Lizzie's heart started to pound. What if *Kate* ended up married to Ethan? Oh, no. That couldn't happen. It just couldn't!

"Larry Tudgeman," Mrs. Stebel finished.

Lizzie had to stifle a giggle as she watched Larry pull his finger out of his nose and give Kate a friendly wave. Larry was a sweet guy, but he was a total superdweeb. He always wore the same putty-colored shirt with the lime green collar, and he rarely found time to wash his hair. Lizzie could practically read the horror on Kate's face as she looked over in Larry's direction. Lizzie and Miranda grinned at each other. This was perfect!

Mr. and Mrs. Larry Tudgeman. Mrs. Kate Tudgeman. Kate Sanders-Tudgeman. It's all good.

"Mrs. Stebel," Kate said as she raised her hand in the air, "I can't be married to Larry." She flashed Larry a look of utter disgust as he happily went back to picking his nose.

Mrs. Stebel looked at Kate from beneath tired lids. "But you *are* married to Larry," she said.

Lizzie and Miranda looked at each other and giggled. Even Gordo was smiling.

"Stop saying that!" Kate insisted. "I want a new husband."

"There are no new husbands, Kate," Mrs. Stebel said patiently. "Now you and Larry come on up here and select your jobs." She pointed to the fishbowl at the edge of her desk.

This is great. I could be married to a tree frog and still have a better marriage than Kate.

Larry and Kate walked up to Mrs. Stebel's desk. They both reached into the fishbowl at the same time. When Kate's hand touched Larry's, she drew it back, then wiped it on Larry's shirt, as if trying to get rid of his cooties. She flipped her long, blond hair over her shoulders disdainfully.

Larry ignored her and pulled a pink slip of paper from the bowl. "Yeah!" he said eagerly as he glanced at the slip of paper. "Hey, I'm a mailman! No, no," he said, deepening his voice, "I'm a mail *delivery*man. For without me, there is no mail. I am the Mail Man." He punched his fist in the air.

Kate sighed and pulled a slip from the bowl. "I'm a TV anchorwoman," she read. Kate's expression changed completely. She smiled, putting her hand to her throat and gazing off into space, as though picturing her brilliant future. "I *love* that!" she said breathlessly.

"Honey, that's so great," Larry said, giving Kate a pat on the shoulder.

Kate slapped Larry's hand away. "Put a cork in it, Tudgeman," she snapped. Then she gave him a haughty look, turned on her heel, and strode back to her seat.

"All right," Mrs. Stebel went on, "Lizzie McGuire?"

Lizzie sat up eagerly and gazed at the back of Ethan's head in an attempt to make him her husband, using the energy of her mind. If only she had that X-Man power!

"Lizzie, you'll be paired with . . ." Mrs. Stebel looked down at her yellow pad.

Ethan Craft, Ethan Craft, Ethan Craft, Ethan Craft, Ethan Craft . . .

". . . David Gordon," Mrs. Stebel read.

The name was so unexpected that, for a

moment, Lizzie wasn't even sure she'd heard it right. Gordo? Lizzie peeked over at her best friend, who looked about as surprised as she felt.

Gordo's cool. Yeah, I'm seein' it. Best friends equals best marriage. Mix those two together and we have a recipe for victory. No paper for us this weekend. Yes!

Gordo waggled his eyebrows at Lizzie, and she giggled as they hauled themselves out from behind their desks and made their way to the career fishbowl.

Lizzie picked first. "Lawyer," she said as she read from her paper. She grinned. "Cool Moe Dee."

Gordo plucked his paper from the bowl. "Sanitation engineer."

Lizzie winced as Gordo groaned, but she couldn't help giggling a little.

"Oh, no, I'm a garbageman," Gordo said. "I'm Gordo the garbageman." He shook his head and turned back toward his desk. "My wife's a lawyer," he said. "I pick up trash."

"Hey." Larry reached out and grabbed Gordo's arm. "It doesn't make you less of a man. Trust me, I know." He pointed to where Kate sat, inspecting her perfect French manicure. "My wife?" Larry whispered. "TV personality."

Gordo rolled his eyes and walked back to his desk.

"Miranda Sanchez," Mrs. Stebel announced, "you'll be paired with Ethan Craft."

Lizzie's mouth dropped open in shock. So did Kate's. And so did Miranda's.

Okay, she's my best friend, so i guess i'm happy for her. But this is so unfair.

Miranda turned to Lizzie, clearly stunned, then walked unsteadily to the front of the class to pull her occupation from the bowl.

Ethan smiled at Miranda as she reached Mrs. Stebel's desk. "Hey, Mrs. Ethan Craft," he said to her casually as he reached toward the fishbowl.

Miranda had to press her lips together to keep from grinning like crazy. She looked over at Lizzie, who gave her a thumbs-up as Ethan pulled a slip of paper from the bowl.

"Surgeon," Ethan read. He looked blankly at Mrs. Stebel. "That's, like, a doctor, right?"

Okay, so i've met vegetables brighter than Ethan. But he is a total hottie.

"He's a doctor," Gordo grumbled in disbelief, "and I'm a garbageman." He dropped his pen on his desk and shook his head.

Miranda looked down at her piece of paper. "Homemaker," she read. She gave a satisfied little shrug, then folded the paper and slipped it into her pocket.

Ethan held out his elbow to Miranda. "Can I escort Mrs. Ethan Craft to her seat?" he asked, flashing her a megawatt smile.

Kate glared at them, pouting, as Ethan walked Miranda back to her desk. Lizzie tried to smile. After all, she didn't want to be like

Kate. She wanted to feel happy for her best friend. Really. But everything about this project was just so unfair!

Miranda laced her arm through Ethan's and grinned. "That's Mrs. *Doctor* Ethan Craft," she corrected him.

Mrs. Doctor Ethan Craft?

Ugh. Things were getting worse by the minute.

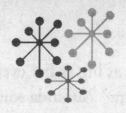

CHAPTER TWO

"Hey!" Miranda called as she walked over to where Lizzie and Gordo were sitting together at their usual table in the atrium. Lizzie looked up and smiled at her friend, but Miranda didn't sit down. "I just wanted to let you guys know I'm eating with my *husband the doctor* today," Miranda said, holding out her hand. Lizzie had to squint. Miranda was wearing the biggest cubic zirconia Lizzie had ever seen. That is, she *hoped* it was a cubic zirconia. It was as big as her eyeball! "See you guys in the gym?" Miranda said as she waggled her fingers in front of Lizzie, then made a face, smiled, and walked away.

"Did you see the rock on Miranda's hand?" Lizzie asked Gordo as Miranda hurried over to where Ethan sat on the other side of the atrium.

Gordo just rolled his eyes.

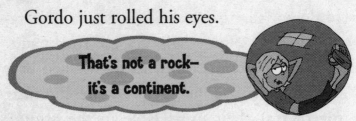

That's not a rock— it's a continent.

"I've been thinking about it," Gordo said, leaning toward Lizzie. "I'm not gonna let the trashman thing get me down."

Lizzie sighed, and peered over at the table where Miranda was sitting next to Ethan. Lizzie felt a pang of jealousy as Ethan laughed at something Miranda said. What could

Miranda have said that was so funny? Lizzie wondered. Ethan should be sitting with me, she thought, laughing at *my* jokes!

Lizzie wished that Gordo would be quiet, so that she could hear what Ethan and Miranda were talking about. But Gordo was on a roll, droning on and on about his career as a sanitation engineer. "And I've got plans," Gordo added. "Big plans. I'm gonna build a trash empire. With employees and trucks and city contracts. It's gonna be huge."

Just then, Lizzie heard a voice behind her. "Hey, Kate?"

Lizzie turned and saw Larry standing next to the queen bee herself. He was holding a cafeteria tray loaded down with today's special: meat loaf and brussels sprouts. I can't believe he got the sprouts, Lizzie thought as she watched Larry stand there, waiting for Kate to notice him.

Kate didn't. She completely ignored Larry, pretending to inspect her perfect French manicure.

"Kate?" Larry said, more loudly this time.

Kate sighed, but didn't even look up at Larry. "Do I know you?" she asked.

"Uh, yeah," Larry replied patiently. "I'm your husband?"

Kate went back to inspecting her nails.

"Mrs. Stebel's class?" Larry went on. "The mailman?" He plopped his tray onto the table and slid into the empty seat next to Kate. "Okay," he said. "We should probably get to work on this."

"Look," Kate said nastily, "I have plans this weekend, so I can't write a paper, so I need the best marriage, which means *you* can't be in it." She put her dainty hand in Larry's face. "Okay?" Kate waved to someone across the cafeteria.

Larry speared something on his plate and held it out to Kate. "Brussels sprout?" he offered.

"Ew!" Kate cried. She moved away from him and flailed at the gross-smelling sprout.

Lizzie laughed. Who knew that brussels sprouts could be put to such good use?

"The key is one truck," Gordo droned on, cutting into Lizzie's people-watching. "Just one garbage truck. And that becomes two garbage trucks."

Lizzie glanced over at Miranda and Ethan again. They were giggling at something. Oh, aren't we just so hilarious today? Lizzie thought jealously.

"Then three," Gordo went on. "Then a lot of garbage trucks. A fleet of garbage trucks. For, you see, trucks equal contracts, and contracts equal money, and money equals power."

Lizzie watched as Ethan offered Miranda a

French fry, and she took it with a shy smile. *Grr.* Is that fair? Lizzie thought. Miranda gets Ethan and French fries, and I have to sit here, listening to Gordo's lecture on the possibilities of garbage?

"Are you even listening to me?" Gordo asked suddenly. He snapped his fingers in front of Lizzie's face. "Hello!" he called.

"Uh. Yeah," Lizzie said vaguely, tearing her eyes away from Dr. and Mrs. Ethan Craft. "You're talking about trash." She glanced over at her best friend, who was smiling as Ethan picked at his lunch.

"You know, Lizzie, I know we're friends, but sometimes I feel like you take me for granted," Gordo said. He leaned in to get her to notice him. "Like *now.*"

Lizzie snapped back to attention. "What?" she asked.

"How do you think that makes me feel?"

Gordo asked. "We've been married for less than a period, and you're already jealous of someone else's husband."

"I'm not jealous!" Lizzie insisted.

"We have to work on this marriage thing together," Gordo told her.

i'm not jealous. She's Mrs. Doctor Ethan Craft. i'm married to a trashman. i am not jealous.

Lizzie nodded. Gordo was right. She knew he was . . . but she couldn't help sneaking just one more look at Miranda and Ethan.

Lizzie was propped on a stool at the kitchen table, doing her homework, when Matt ran into the kitchen. He yanked open the fridge, grabbed some root beer and beef jerky, and stuffed them into a small red cooler. Then he slammed the fridge closed and ran out onto the patio. Lizzie didn't even look up. More weirdness from her brother—and she did not want to get involved.

"Honey?" Mrs. McGuire called after Matt as she walked into the kitchen. He ignored her, so she turned to Lizzie. "Lizzie?" her mom said in a low voice as she leaned against the table where Lizzie was working. "Do you know where your brother's going?"

"Mom," Lizzie said, lifting her eyebrows. "I'm his sister. We don't talk."

"I'm just worried," Lizzie's mom said absently as she watched Matt out on the patio. "He's been really good lately. But, like, *too* good. Are you sure you haven't noticed anything weird?"

"Hmm." Lizzie pretended to think for a moment. "Besides his troll-like appearance and his distaste for hygiene, no. Anyway, I've got enough to worry about. Miranda gets to be Mrs. Doctor Ethan Craft, and I get to be married to Gordo, the trash king."

Mrs. McGuire gaped at her daughter.

"Oh, school project," Lizzie explained. "Don't worry."

Lizzie's mom planted her hands on her hips. "Listen," she said, "I don't know what your teacher is telling you, but marriage is not about how much you earn or what you have. It's about love." She put her hand across her heart. "And trust. And communication. Right, honey?" she asked as Lizzie's dad walked into the kitchen and grabbed an apple from the fruit bowl.

"Huh?" Mr. McGuire said as he polished the apple on his shirt.

"Just say yes," Mrs. McGuire told him.

"Yes," Mr. McGuire said obediently.

Mrs. McGuire gave her husband a peck on the cheek. "Good boy."

Okay. Nice that my parents like each other. But gross when they kiss in front of me.

"I'm so outta here," Lizzie said as she flipped her notebook shut. She grimaced as she walked out of the kitchen, leaving her lovebird parents to smooch it up in her absence.

"Honey, I'm worried about Matt," Mrs. McGuire said as she watched Matt gather his things and leave the patio. "I think you should go follow him."

"I'll get my coat," Mr. McGuire said, putting his apple back on the counter. He grabbed his jacket from a peg in the hall, hurried outside, and followed his son across the backyard and through a wide field until he came to some woods. Mr. McGuire had to dodge branches and leaves as he followed his son's path through the thick trees. After a few minutes, Matt seemed to disappear. Mr. McGuire was about to give up and turn back when he noticed a large hole in the side of a hill. A shower of dirt came flying out of it.

Mr. McGuire peered into the hole, just as a pile of dirt landed in his face. Mr. McGuire spat the soil out of his mouth and crawled deeper into the cave, just as another pile of dirt smacked him in the face. He shook his head and crawled into the hole, which, it turned out, was a cave large enough to stand up in. Matt was in one corner, wearing a baseball cap with a flashlight duct-taped to the front, shoveling dirt.

"Matt?" Mr. McGuire called as he crawled into the cave. "Hey, Matt. Hi." He gave Matt a little wave. "What are you doing here?"

Matt looked surprised to see his father. "Uh. Tidying up my cave," he explained uncomfortably.

Mr. McGuire looked around, still on his knees, as he brushed the dirt from his clothes. "Is that what this is?"

"Uh. Yeah," Matt said.

"I didn't know there was a cave up here," Mr. McGuire said. He adjusted his glasses, which had been knocked askew by the dirt.

"There wasn't," Matt told him.

Mr. McGuire's eyebrows flew up as he gazed at his son. "You mean, you made this cave?"

"I dug it," Matt said.

Mr. McGuire looked around, clearly impressed. The cave was pretty big. "Wow," he said. "Well, how long did it take you?"

"I dunno." Matt shrugged. "Couple of weeks?"

Mr. McGuire looked around again, this time, in confusion. "Why?" he asked.

"Well, you see, I ran into these rocks," Matt said, pointing behind him.

"No, Matt." Mr. McGuire shook his head. "What I mean is, why did you dig a cave?"

"Dad, haven't you ever wanted a place that's your own?" Matt asked. "A place you can just hang?"

Mr. McGuire thought about that for a moment. "Each and every day of my life, son," he admitted.

"Are you gonna tell Mom?" Matt asked.

"Well," Mr. McGuire said, "you have parental supervision, so that would make this okay."

Matt and his dad looked at each other for a moment. Then Matt smiled and handed his dad a shovel. "Welcome to the Matt Cave," he said.

CHAPTER THREE

Lizzie headed over to her favorite cybercafé, the Digital Bean, to study. While I'm here, I might as well get one of their delicious Superberry smoothies, Lizzie thought as she went up to the counter and placed her order with the lanky, dark-haired waitress. There was no point in studying on an empty stomach. While she waited for the drink, Lizzie scouted around for a place to sit. Suddenly, her eye fell on a couple in the corner who looked very cozy. The girl flipped her hair, and Lizzie felt her stomach drop. She knew those two!

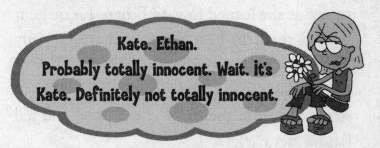

Kate. Ethan.
Probably totally innocent. Wait. it's Kate. Definitely not totally innocent.

Kate leaned flirtatiously toward Ethan and took a sip from the smoothie they were sharing. Lizzie frowned. This did not look good. She had to find out what was going on!

Lizzie spotted a garbage can behind Kate and Ethan. Thinking fast, she grabbed a tray filled with empty plates and used cups and napkins and oh-so-casually made her way over toward the garbage can, which was conveniently hidden behind a column between her and Kate. Garbage is really the theme of my life lately, Lizzie thought, as she peered around the column to get a look at the cozy couple.

"So what I was thinking . . ." Kate started to say, as she leaned toward Ethan. Lizzie bent toward them to hear more, and accidentally tipped over the tray she was holding. One of the drinks spilled, and when Lizzie tried to step away from the mess, she slipped and fell flat on her back!

Unbelievably, Kate was so wrapped up in Ethan that she didn't even notice. "I was thinking that Mrs. Stebel clearly made a mistake with my marriage. So I'm planning to leave Larry at the reunion."

Lizzie hauled herself off the floor and crawled around the column until she was under Kate and Ethan's table. Ugh. Now she had a gorgeous view of Kate's perfect pedicure, and of the gum stuck to the underside of the table.

Ethan thought about this for a moment. "Does that mean I get . . . two wives?" he asked eagerly.

"No," Kate said slowly. "But if you leave Miranda, then you and I could be married."

What? Lizzie couldn't believe what she was hearing. Kate was going to double-cross her own husband—and Miranda! But would Ethan go along with it? Even though she knew that Ethan and Kate could discover her at any minute, Lizzie couldn't leave yet.

Still, the floor was a very uncomfortable place to sit. She adjusted her position so that she was leaning against the table leg, and hit her head against the underside of the table. Ouch! Now her head hurt, and her hair was caught in a gross wad of used chewing gum! Mega-ick! And even worse—how was she going to ever get out from under this table without ripping half of the hair out of her head?

"Oh," Ethan said finally. "That's still cool."

Lizzie tried to pull her hair out of the gum, but it wouldn't budge. It was like it was stuck there with industrial cement or something!

"How's that sound, Dr. Craft?" Kate asked craftily.

Ethan laughed. "You're really smart," he said.

Just then, the lanky waitress stepped out from behind the counter and peered around the café. Please, don't let her see me, Lizzie begged silently. Please!

Spotting Lizzie under the counter, the waitress walked over and delivered Lizzie's smoothie. "Excuse me," the waitress said, leaning under the table, "here's your drink."

Lizzie grimaced, then took the drink. After all, what choice did she have? Thanks to the gum, she was permanently stuck to this table. Just stay cool, Lizzie told herself. Maybe nobody will notice. "Thanks."

Kate and Ethan peered under the table. Lizzie winced, then smiled at them feebly. "Hi," she said, and took a sip of her drink, as though she liked to hang out underneath café tables all the time.

i would give a year's allowance to be anyplace but here right now. Maybe two years'.

"Garbage is gold," Gordo said as he scribbled something onto a piece of paper. "Stinky gold, but gold nonetheless."

"Whatever." Lizzie flopped backward onto the couch in her family's living room. Gordo had been talking nonstop about garbage for the past ten minutes. He had come over to her house to work on their marriage project, which was quickly turning into the David

Gordon Trashtacular. He had brought a ton of notes and articles, all about the sanitation industry. In Lizzie's opinion, Gordo had a serious case of trash on the brain.

"C'mon, Lizzie," Gordo begged, "give me a hand here." He gestured toward his garbage notes. "I mean—you want the perfect marriage, and you've been making zero effort."

"Gordo, quit nagging me!" Lizzie griped.

"*Nagging* you?" Gordo repeated, as though he couldn't believe what Lizzie had just said. "I wouldn't have to nag you if you paid attention to me."

"I'd pay attention to you if you talked about something other than garbage," Lizzie snapped back.

"Like what?" Gordo asked patiently.

"Ethan and Miranda," Lizzie said.

Gordo nodded, as though he understood perfectly. "Mmm."

Lizzie rolled her eyes. What was that "*mmm*" noise supposed to mean? She knew that Gordo just thought that Lizzie was bummed because she would rather be Mrs. Dr. Ethan Craft than Mrs. Garbage-Obsession. But that wasn't the problem at all! Well, it wasn't the *entire* problem.

"You know trash might not be glamorous, Lizzie," Gordo said, "but it's gonna put our kids through school."

"That's not it," Lizzie said impatiently.

"Then what is it?" Gordo asked.

"I went to the Digital Bean yesterday and I saw Ethan—with *Kate*," Lizzie explained. "Kate's planning to leave Larry at the reunion. And she wants Ethan to do the same to Miranda."

Gordo frowned. "But it's just a school project," he said. "It's not real."

"It'll be real to Miranda when she gets

dumped in front of the entire class," Lizzie pointed out.

"Okay. You're right," Gordo admitted. "We have to tell her before the reunion."

Lizzie looked at the ceiling. "How do we do that?"

"You have to talk to her," Gordo said gently.

Lizzie sighed. Gordo was right, and she knew it. There was only one problem. How in the world was Lizzie going to tell Miranda?

"There's a bunch of batteries in the garage," Mr. McGuire said as he and Matt hurried into the kitchen, "and I think there's more beef jerky in the pantry."

"Hey!" Mrs. McGuire called, jogging after them.

Mr. McGuire and Matt stopped in their tracks as Mrs. McGuire gaped at the mud and dirt caked all over their clothes.

"Sam," Mrs. McGuire said slowly, "can I talk to you for a second?"

"Sure," Mr. McGuire replied. He leaned toward Matt and whispered something in his ear.

"Got it," Matt said and scurried out of the kitchen.

Mr. McGuire turned back to his wife and grinned at her innocently.

"What's going on?" Mrs. McGuire asked. Her eyebrows drew together.

"Nothing," Mr. McGuire said quickly. "Just a little male-bonding time. With me and Matt." He cleared his throat uncomfortably, then turned and strode out of the room.

Mrs. McGuire stared after him for a moment, clearly confused. "You know I'm gonna find out!" she called after him. But her husband was already long gone.

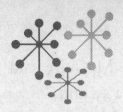

CHAPTER FOUR

Lizzie glanced around the Digital Bean. When she'd called Miranda's house earlier, her mom had said that Miranda was at the cyber-café. Lizzie and Gordo had hurried over there so that Lizzie could break the lousy 4–1–1 about Kate and Ethan's plan. But half of Lizzie was hoping that her friend wouldn't be there. She hated giving people bad news.

Suddenly, Lizzie spotted a familiar-looking head of dark hair. Miranda was sitting at a table by herself. It's now or never, Lizzie thought as she hurried over. She wanted to get this heinous conversation over with as quickly as possible. "Hey, Miranda!" Lizzie said as she slid into the empty chair across from her friend. "Haven't seen you around."

"Yeah, being a doctor's wife can be pretty hectic," Miranda said with a smile. She took a sip from her drink and put it back on the table.

Lizzie giggled nervously. "So," she said uncomfortably, "how's that working for you?" She couldn't help noticing that Miranda was doing something new with her hair. She looked really good. She probably did it to impress Ethan, Lizzie thought, stifling a flash of anger. How could Ethan treat her friend this way? It wasn't fair—not when Miranda was so sweet and nice and fun.

"We've decided that Ethan's a heart surgeon,"

Miranda said, grinning. "We have three kids: Britney, Gwyneth, and Ethan Junior. I drive the kids to soccer practice in my metallic-blue SUV with beige leather interior." Miranda lifted her eyebrows and sat back in her chair, smiling at her fantasy.

"And what about Ethan?" Lizzie asked.

Miranda shrugged. "Oh, he works a lot. Heart surgeons do, you know. But he'll meet me here later." She picked up her soda and took a small sip. "This project is so much fun."

"Great," Lizzie lied. She pressed her lips together, wishing that she could just duck out of there. Miranda looked so happy. Lizzie didn't want to be the one to ruin her best friend's perfect fantasy life, complete with an SUV and kids with trendy names. But if she didn't tell Miranda what was really going on, Lizzie would just have to watch Miranda's life come crashing down around her in Mrs. Stebel's class. I have to tell her the truth, Lizzie decided. Right now. "Miranda," Lizzie said miserably, "I have to tell you something—"

"Hey, ladies!" a voice cried, interrupting Lizzie. "Dr. E's in the house!" Lizzie looked up just in time to see Ethan striding toward them. He settled onto the stool beside Miranda, who giggled happily.

i am so erasing his name from my notebook.

"Sorry I'm late," Ethan said to Miranda. "I had some doctor stuff to do," he joked, putting finger-quotation marks around the word "doctor." Lizzie had to bite her lip to keep from telling him that she'd hoped he'd been giving himself a personality transplant.

Miranda nodded at Ethan, then turned back to Lizzie. "You were saying, Lizzie?" she asked.

Miranda smiled at her, expectantly. Lizzie glanced uncomfortably at Ethan, then turned back to Miranda. Just tell her, Lizzie thought. Tell her now! "Um. I was saying . . . that I'm meeting Gordo here, so, I have to go." Lizzie shoved back her chair and walked away quickly.

i'm not a coward. Really. it's just not the right time.

Oh, help! Lizzie thought as she joined Gordo by the snack counter.

"I hope you guys are as happy as we are!" Miranda called, waving at Lizzie and Gordo.

Gordo shot Lizzie a dubious look. "She, uh, doesn't look too upset," he said hopefully.

Lizzie groaned in frustration. "That's because she doesn't know," she snapped. She glanced over at her friend, who was grinning widely at Ethan. "I couldn't tell her," Lizzie admitted. "I mean, she looks so *happy*."

"You know, the longer you wait, the more hurt she's going to get," Gordo pointed out.

i'm such a wimp.

"You're right," Lizzie said. She shook her head. "I just don't know how I'm going to break it to her."

Gordo patted Lizzie on the shoulder. "You'll think of something," he said.

Lizzie sighed. She sure hoped that he was right.

Meanwhile, back at the cave, Mr. McGuire and Matt were munching on string cheese and reclining on beach chairs. Mr. McGuire was wearing an old football helmet with a flashlight duct-taped to the front, while Matt had on his baseball cap/flashlight headgear. They had spent the afternoon making a few cave drawings with sidewalk chalk—until the art project turned into a duel with chalk sabers. Then they had guzzled root beer until Matt complained he had a stomachache. After that, they lit a bunch of little candles around the cave and sat down to relax in their cheery glow.

"Dad, does it get much better than this?" Matt asked with a contented sigh. He tossed a rubber ball in the air, then caught it again.

"Nope," Mr. McGuire said between bites of string cheese. "It doesn't." He looked around the cave. "You know, I've been thinking. What we really need is some more room."

Matt lifted his eyebrows. "Talk to me."

Mr. McGuire pointed to a spot just behind Matt. "I could blow that wall out another seven feet. Then we'd have enough room in here for a generator. We could have indoor lights."

"And TV," Matt added. "Can't forget TV."

"Yeah, TV'd be cool," Mr. McGuire agreed. He looked around, then up at the ceiling. "We could probably punch a hole in the roof here . . . bring in some satellite."

"Cool!" Matt smiled at his dad.

"How big a screen do you think we could get in here?" Mr. McGuire mused.

"Sam? Matt!" Mr. McGuire looked over, and saw Mrs. McGuire's head poking into the entrance to their secret lair! "What are you guys doing in there?" she demanded. "Get out of this mud hole, right now."

"But—" Matt and Mr. McGuire chorused.

"No, no buts," Mrs. McGuire said, cutting them off. She shook her head. "This thing could collapse on you any minute! Come on."

"But it's cool!" Matt complained.

"I know it's cool, honey," Mrs. McGuire replied, "but it's dangerous." She looked at her husband. "Right, Sam?"

Mr. McGuire sighed.

"Right, Sam?" Mrs. McGuire prompted again.

Mr. McGuire thought for a moment, then

turned to Matt. "Son," he said, "she caught us fair and square. At this point, resistance is futile." He turned off the flashlight strapped to his helmet, as a signal of defeat.

"Women," Matt said sadly. "You can't live with 'em—you can't let 'em know where your cave is."

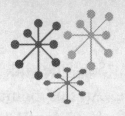

CHAPTER FIVE

"I cannot believe you're wearing that," Lizzie said to Gordo. She frowned at the dirty pair of garbage-green overalls he had on. Gordo's fashion taste usually ran to the extreme, but an authentic garbageman outfit was a bit much, even for Gordo.

Gordo and Lizzie were standing together in the gym, which Mrs. Stebel had decorated with balloons and a big banner that read MRS. STEBEL'S 20TH CLASS REUNION. Mrs. Stebel had gone all out for the occasion. She had even laid out little sandwiches and a big bowl of punch on a long table at the rear of the gym. All of the students were dressed up in costumes to represent their careers. Lizzie was wearing a dark blue suit, and had her hair pulled back neatly in what she thought of as a "lawyerly" do. But did Gordo really have to go totally all out?

"I'm a trashman," Gordo protested as he looked down at his coveralls. "I'm proud of where I come from."

Lizzie shook her head. She had hoped that her husband would have dressed up for the occasion—maybe even worn a suit. After all, wasn't he supposed to be the *head* of a garbage empire? Did he really have to dress like he'd just finished having lunch with Oscar the Grouch? "Don't you care if we win?" Lizzie asked.

"No, I don't," Gordo admitted. "Not any-more."

Lizzie looked at him, hugging her notebook against her chest. What is Gordo talking about? she wondered. He'd been working hard on this project all week. He *had* to care!

"I care that ever since we got married, you just seem annoyed by me," Gordo went on. "I care that I feel like my best friend is taking me for granted."

Lizzie sighed. Gordo was right—as usual. She really hadn't been a very good friend to him. What is up with me lately? Lizzie wondered, thinking about how she'd failed Miranda the day before.

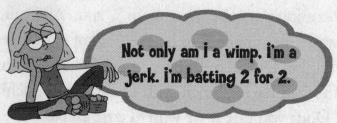

A movement caught Lizzie's eye, and she turned to see Miranda walk into the gym with

Ethan. Miranda was wearing a housedress and apron, and even had a kerchief over her dark hair. Ethan was in mint-green scrubs. Miranda folded her arms across her chest as she listened to Frankie Wallis and Sally Falconer finish up their report. Frankie was dressed as a farmer, while Sally had on police blues.

"So, basically, while I was out milking cows, she was in the big city, fightin' crime. . . ." Frankie explained.

"But I was home on weekends," Sally went on, "and we had three kids."

Lizzie wasn't paying attention to the report. Her eyes were locked on Ethan and Miranda. She saw Ethan waggle his eyebrows at someone, and turned just in time to see Kate give him a conspiratorial wave. Lizzie narrowed her eyes.

"Commuter marriage," Mrs. Stebel said, nodding appreciatively at Frankie and Sally.

"Interesting." She looked down at her clip-board. "So, next up we have Kate Sanders and Larry Tudgeman," she announced.

Kate turned and daintily made her way to the stage. Lizzie frowned at her. Kate was wearing a pink suit and carrying a fake micro-phone. She had even teased her hair until she looked like a beauty pageant contestant after electroshock therapy. It was some serious helmet hair. Larry had on a regulation U.S. Postal Service outfit, complete with pith helmet and messenger bag stuffed with mail. Lizzie had to hand it to Larry—his outfit looked completely authentic. She couldn't help wondering if he had made it himself. Or maybe he'd just bribed a mailman.

Onstage, Larry leaned in toward the micro-phone, but Kate snatched it away from him. "I left Larry the day after our wedding," she announced snidely. "Of course, there were no children. I replaced Katie Couric on the *Today* show and won several Emmys. I lived fabulously ever after," she said, gesturing grandly. Larry gaped at her as she went on, "The end. Do I win?" Kate turned to Mrs. Stebel and smiled eagerly.

"Uh, I do not remember agreeing to any of that," Larry said into the microphone.

Kate sighed, throwing her head back dramatically, as though a husband as nerdy as hers couldn't possibly be asked to remember anything.

Lizzie winced. This was way embarrassing—and she wasn't even Larry's friend! Lizzie sneaked a glance at Miranda, who looked like she couldn't believe what a witch Kate was being.

"Kate, Larry, I want to see you after the presentations, please," Mrs. Stebel said stiffly. She frowned at Kate for a moment, clearly not amused, then looked back at her clipboard. "After a five-minute break, next up will be Miranda Sanchez and Ethan Craft."

Miranda put down her glass of punch and grabbed Ethan's arm eagerly. He quickly finished chewing the mini-sandwich he had just stuffed into his mouth and followed Miranda as she led the way toward the stage.

Lizzie took a deep breath. She couldn't let this happen. She couldn't let Miranda get dumped the way Larry had been! Not when she could stop it. Lizzie started after her friend.

"Wait." Gordo held out his hand in a stop gesture. "Where are you going?"

"To tell her," Lizzie explained. "I have to. I can't let her be humiliated in front of the entire class. I mean, sure, she's been Mrs. Doctor Ethan Craft for a week. But Miranda's been my friend for much longer. I can't just let her walk into this." Gordo nodded, and Lizzie hurried after Miranda.

"Hey, Miranda," Lizzie said quickly, as she stepped in front of Miranda, "can I talk to you for a sec?"

"Can't it wait?" Miranda asked, glancing toward the stage. "I'm about to give my report."

"No," Lizzie said firmly, "it can't."

Miranda turned to Ethan. "Give us a sec."

"Sure thing, sweetheart," Ethan said, giving her a sly wink. Miranda blew Ethan a little kiss. Ugh, Lizzie thought, as she watched Ethan amble toward the stage. This whole situation is enough to make me lose my lunch.

"Okay, Miranda," Lizzie said in a low voice, "Ethan is going to leave you. Like, now."

Miranda crossed her arms and narrowed her eyes. "Just because you're jealous doesn't give you the right to make stuff up," she said angrily.

"Miranda, I'm not making it up," Lizzie said earnestly. "I'm your friend."

"Yeah?" Miranda said angrily. "Some friend you are."

"Some friend *I* am?" Lizzie demanded, gesturing toward smarmy Ethan and his stupid doctor outfit. "One lame school project and you're spending all your time waiting around for some guy who doesn't even care about you, and who's going to leave you and embarrass you in front of the entire class!"

"What are you talking about?" Miranda asked, giving her hair a little flip. "Ethan and I spend tons of time together."

"No," Lizzie replied. "Ethan spends a ton of time with *Kate*."

Miranda's mouth fell open, and she seemed to deflate a bit.

Lizzie bit her lip, but she knew that she had to force herself to go on. Miranda needed to know the whole story. "I saw them at the Digital Bean together," Lizzie explained. "Kate asked Ethan to leave you at the reunion, just like she left Larry." Miranda looked as though she had just been punched in the stomach. Lizzie hated hurting her friend, but what else could she do? "I tried to tell you," Lizzie said apologetically, "but you seemed so happy."

"What?" Miranda asked. Her voice was thick with emotion. "How?"

Lizzie shook her head. "I'm really sorry."

"Yo! Is there a Mrs. Doctor in the house?" Ethan said into the microphone.

Slowly, Miranda turned to face the stage. She looked a little sick. She hesitated a moment, then squared her shoulders and walked toward her "husband."

Lizzie's heart was aching. She wished that she could do something for her friend. But she had just done the only thing she could. The rest was up to Miranda.

Ethan leaned toward the mike as Miranda took the stage. "Me and Miranda had our, uh, issues," he said into the microphone. "Y'know, like on *Ricki Lake*."

"Ethan was a heart surgeon," Miranda added mechanically. "I was a housewife. We had three kids. Britney, Gwyneth, and Ethan Junior. We had a vacation house. A swimming pool." She looked down at the floor. "I thought we had a pretty good life," she added quietly.

Ethan reached for the microphone, but Miranda snatched it away from him. "But Ethan was seeing someone else," she said angrily. "Weren't you, Ethan?" She narrowed her eyes at him accusingly.

"Uh, no," Ethan hedged. He turned pale, and Lizzie was pretty sure he was remembering all of the afternoons he had spent with Kate.

Miranda ignored him. "Ethan was going to leave me for Kate," she explained to the class. "But, you see, *Doctor*, that's not how I operate. I'm leaving you." Miranda poked Ethan in the chest. "You can take the car, you can take everything, but you can't take my *dignity*. I can't be married to someone who can't even manage to be my friend." Miranda threw the microphone on the floor and ran out of the room.

Ethan stood there, dumbfounded.

Lizzie felt like clapping. Miranda had totally made Ethan look like the jerk he had been!

There was a small shriek of feedback as Ethan picked up the microphone. "Uh . . . *Kate*?" he asked, frowning in confusion. "I thought I was gonna have *two* wives. . . . Now I've got none."

Lizzie rolled her eyes, and looked around to see Kate's reaction. But Kate wasn't even paying attention to Ethan. She was too busy griping at Larry over by the punch bowl.

"Kate, we need to go talk to Mrs. Stebel," Larry said.

"You better keep your mouth shut and agree that all of our decisions were mutual," Kate said, pointing a finger in Larry's face. "I'm *not* writing a report because you're a lousy husband." She jabbed him in the shoulder, knocking his hat askew.

"Oh, I'm a lousy husband?" Larry said, snatching his hat from his head. "Well, maybe if you'd just worked with me on this like I asked and the rules said, we wouldn't have this problem."

"Fine." Kate sneered. "I'll work with you. This marriage is over. How's that work for you?" She turned her back on Larry and folded her arms across her chest. "Now pour me some punch," she commanded.

Larry stared at the floor a minute, clearly stunned. "Yeah," he said finally, sighing in resignation. "Yeah, I'll pour you some punch." He placed his helmet on the refreshment table and took the ladle out of the punch bowl. Then he hauled the bowl off the table . . . and dumped the punch all over Kate! Sticky red punch splashed all over Kate's giant hairdo, deflating it, and dribbled all over her pink suit. The class cracked up as Kate stood there, soggy and humiliated, wiping gummy strands of hair off her face. It was the first time that Lizzie had ever seen Kate completely speechless!

"*Now* this marriage is over," Larry announced. He patted Kate on the back, then walked out of the gym.

Gordo turned to Lizzie. "I guess that's the

risk you take when you marry a postal worker," he said.

Lizzie winced, but she had to laugh. Witnessing Kate get her comeuppance from the Tudge was priceless. This was sure to cheer up Miranda!

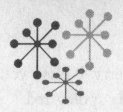

CHAPTER SIX

"I can't believe Ethan was gonna leave me," Miranda said over the phone later that night. She sounded pretty bummed. "It had to happen, right?"

"Yeah," Lizzie and Gordo agreed gently. Lizzie and her best buds were having their usual three-way, school-night chat. Even though Lizzie felt bad for Miranda, she was glad that things were back to normal with her friends.

"Well, I'm sorry I blew you guys off for Ethan," Miranda apologized.

"Well, now you know who your real friends are," Gordo pointed out.

"That was some speech you gave, Miranda," Lizzie added, hoping that it would make her friend feel better.

"Yeah, well," Miranda said, "I have my real friends to thank for that."

"I can't believe you didn't win," Lizzie went on.

"I *know*," Miranda agreed. "And I never thought the cop and the farmer would take it."

"A commuter marriage," Gordo scoffed. "How difficult was that? I mean, Lizzie, you and I, we had some real issues that we worked through."

"And we still have five hundred words due on Monday," Lizzie complained. Ugh. It was so unfair!

"So, what are you guys gonna write?" Miranda wanted to know.

"I think I might write about not taking people for granted," Lizzie said, "and being really lucky when you can marry your best friend."

"Oh, great, you realize this *now*?" Gordo demanded. "Where was that a couple of hours ago? We could've won with that!"

"Yeah, well, I'm waiting a really, really long time before I get married," Miranda said.

"Yeah," Lizzie agreed. "I think we're too young to even *pretend* we're married."

"I agree," Gordo said seriously. "But my trash empire could have been something big."

Lizzie gaped at the phone. There was silence at the other end. Miranda was clearly speechless, too.

"Hello?" Gordon's voice barked from the receiver. "Hello?"

Lizzie clicked off, giggling. She knew that Miranda would do the same. "Guys," Lizzie said, shaking her head.

Gordo stared at his receiver, wondering why his best friends had just hung up. "Chicks," he said with a sigh.

Lizzie grinned at the receiver. Even if she and Gordo hadn't won the marriage project, she was glad that she had friends as cool as Miranda and Gordo.

That was the most important thing, anyway. By a long shot.

GET INSIDE HER HEAD

Lizzie McGUiRE

A Disney Channel Original Series

Weekends

Watch it on

© Disney

Visit Lizzie @ DisneyChannel.com

Disney's

KiM POSSIBLE

Saving the world on a school night.

Watch Kim Possible every week day on Disney Channel

DISNEY
CHANNEL

disney.co.uk/disneychannel